PUFFIN

PUGWASH AND

an

PUGWASH AND THE FANCY-DRESS PARTY

'Muttering midships!' cried Pugwash. 'What is the meaning of this!'

'This', replied the Mate, 'is a mutiny! *We* are taking over the ship.'

When Captain Pugwash is cast ashore with his cabin boy, Tom, things soon start to go wrong for the crew, especially when the terrible Cut-throat Jake and his nasty crew turn up unexpectedly.

And when Pugwash plans a Fancy-dress Ball that will fill the empty treasure chest, a group of uninvited 'guests' threaten to ruin everything. Thank goodness for Tom, the clever cabin boy!

Two stories in one book, full of fun and piracy!

John Ryan was born in Edinburgh, though he spent most of his early life in Turkey and French Morocco. After leaving the army he became Assistant Art Master at Harrow, where, he says, the Art Master taught him more about drawing than anyone else before or since. He then went freelance and created his most famous character, Captain Pugwash. The Captain has won the hearts of people all over the world through his television adventures and through his books. John Ryan is married with three children and lives in Sussex.

PUGWASH AND THE MUTINY

and

PUGWASH AND THE FANCY-DRESS PARTY

John Ryan

[signature]

Puffin Books

PUFFIN BOOKS

Published by the Penguin Group
Penguin Books Ltd, 27 Wrights Lane, London W8 5TZ, England
Penguin Books USA Inc., 375 Hudson Street, New York, New York 10014, USA
Penguin Books Australia Ltd, Ringwood, Victoria, Australia
Penguin Books Canada Ltd, 10 Alcorn Avenue, Toronto, Ontario, Canada M4V 3B2
Penguin Books (NZ) Ltd, 182–190 Wairau Road, Auckland 10, New Zealand

Penguin Books Ltd, Registered Offices: Harmondsworth, Middlesex, England

Captain Pugwash and the Mutiny
first published by The Bodley Head Ltd 1982
Pugwash and the Fancy-Dress Party
first published by The Bodley Head Ltd 1982
Published in one volume by Puffin Books 1985
7 9 10 8

Printed in England by Clays Ltd, St Ives plc
Set in Ehrhardt

PUGWASH
AND THE
MUTINY

The ISLAND

N W E S

Later they carried the dinghy to here

Tom's Look-out

The "Flying Dustman" anchored here

Rocky Point

The "Black Pig" anchored here

Jake's pirates came this way

It was quite early in the morning, and the *Black Pig* lay at anchor in the shelter of a little rocky bay, by an island far away in the blue Pacific ocean.

On any other day Captain Pugwash and his pirates would still have been fast asleep, but this morning was different. The Captain had decided to smarten up his ship and his crew. Everybody had been called early, and even Captain Pugwash was up and dressed and sitting in his cabin sipping the early morning tea which Tom the cabin boy had brought him.

He was also putting the finishing touches to a large notice which he had written out. In fact he had just signed his name at the bottom when there was a knock on his door and the Mate came in looking rather uncomfortable.

"Beggin' pardon Cap'n," said he, "but the crew 'as a complaint. The ship's biscuits is hunfit for 'uman consumption. They're full of weevils!"

"Wallopping whales! What on *earth* is a weevil?" asked the Captain.

"They're like small beetles, Cap'n," said Tom. "They eat biscuits."

"In that case," said Pugwash crossly, "the crew had better eat them quickly— or there won't be any biscuits left."

"Sorry, Cap'n, the men won't touch 'em," said the Mate. "They reckon it's cruelty to weevils!"

At this stage, the Captain became very angry.

"Doddering dolphins, Master Mate," he cried. "Pirates should be desperadoes—not do-gooders! Take this notice and nail it to the main mast immediately! Things are going to be very different aboard this ship from now on!"

So the Mate took the notice and nailed it to the mast . . .

but when Barnabas and Willy read it, they were filled with horror and dismay . . .

and when *he* read it, so was the Mate . . .

For a time they muttered angrily together.
Then . . .

straight into the middle of the
Captain's breakfast . . .

marched the three pirates.

"Muttering midships!" cried Pugwash.

"*What* is the meaning of this!"

"This", replied the Mate,
"is a mutiny! *We* are taking
over the ship."

"Aye," chortled Willy,
"we're all captains now!"

"And you are goin'
to be marooned on the
island," growled Barnabas.

"Hexactly!" said the Mate. "Tom lad
. . . pack up the Captain's kit and load it
on the dinghy. He's leaving!"

Poor Captain Pugwash!

He muttered and spluttered a lot . . .

but in the end . . .
he saw that his
crew's mind was made
up . . . and so . . .
complaining bitterly, he
let Tom pack up his
possessions . . .
and got into the dinghy.
The crew handed down his
sea-chest, and supplies of
fresh water, and food, and
pistols and cutlasses and all the
things a castaway would need.

"That's the lot then," said the Mate,
when everything was stowed aboard. "Bye
bye, Cap'n!"

But Tom said, "Hang on, Cap'n. Make
room for me!"

"For who?" asked
Barnabas in a
shocked voice.

"For me,
of course," said Tom.
"After all, I am his cabin boy . . . Bye all!"

And in spite of horrified protests from
the pirates, he climbed down into the dinghy
and started to row towards the island.

"Well, who would 'ave thought it?"
said Pirate Willy, as they watched the
little boat moving further and further
away from the *Black Pig*. They weren't
too worried about doing without their
Captain, but losing Tom was a disaster.

Then the Mate pulled himself together.
"It's no good crying over lost cabin
boys," he announced. "Hoist the main
sail, Cap'n Barnabas, and you Cap'n
Willy, you get the anchor up. And I'll
make us all a nice cup of tea!"

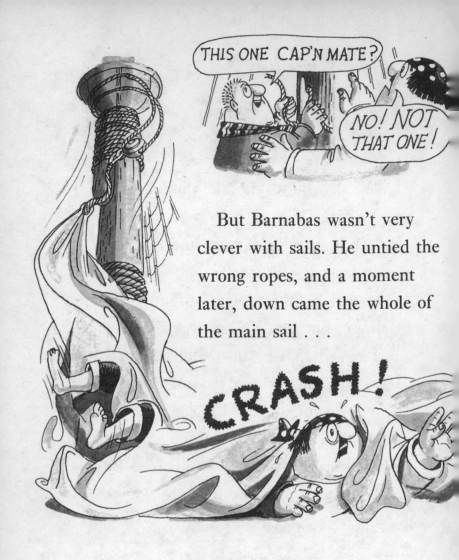

But Barnabas wasn't very
clever with sails. He untied the
wrong ropes, and a moment
later, down came the whole of
the main sail . . .

and the two pirates found themselves
covered in a mass of heaving canvas.

Willy didn't fare much
better with the anchor.
While trying to work out
how best to pull it up, he
leant too far over,

and lost his balance and landed with a
heavy splash in the warm wet water!

"Never mind," thought Willy, as he climbed up the anchor chain, "at least there'll be a nice hot cup o'tea soon."

But when he did get back on deck, and when the other two pirates had unwrapped themselves . . . the Mate shook his head sadly. "No tea," said he. "I've just remembered . . . Tom took the kettle with him!"

For the pirates, it was the start of a very bad day.

They couldn't sail the ship without
Tom to tell them what to do; they didn't
know how to cook, because Tom had
always done that, too. So they were
reduced to eating the despised ship's
biscuits, weevils and all, and that evening
they climbed miserably into their unmade
bunks . . . without even
their bedtime cocoa to
lull them to sleep.

But . . . *much, much* worse was to follow . . .

For that evening, unknown to anyone, *another* pirate ship had arrived at the island and dropped anchor, out of sight, around the point, in another little bay.

It was Cut-throat Jake's ship, and Cut-throat Jake was the most terrible pirate afloat, and by far Captain Pugwash's worst and most frightening enemy.

Even now, Jake and his hideous crew, with muffled oars, were setting off in their longboat to attack the *Black Pig*.

The moon was just rising and Jake rubbed his great hairy hands and growled,

HA-HARRH !

FLYING DUSTMAN

"Dunno why we bothers to muffle them oars! That old rapscallion Pugwash and his useless crew will be snorin' their fat 'eads off by now. And oh-ho-ho—have they got an ugly shock comin'!"

But Jake was wrong about the Captain.
Far away out of sight on the island, he
and Tom were very snug. While Pugwash
had spent the day pottering about on the
island looking for
buried treasure,

here . . .

there . . .

and
everywhere,

Tom had built a small hut out of
bamboo and palm leaves.

Earlier that evening, he had cooked
a delicious dinner, and now Captain
Pugwash was savouring a fine old
French brandy before going to bed.

In fact, he was just turning in for
the night . . .

. . . as Jake's longboat
slid silently under the
bows of the *Black Pig*,
and he and his men
scrambled stealthily up
the anchor chain to
the deck.

"You take the crew,
me beauties," whispered
Jake with an evil grin.

"I'll handle my old friend, the Captain!"

It was indeed an ugly
surprise for the Mate,
Barnabas and Willy when
they woke. Each opened his
eyes to find a gleaming dagger at
his throat, and within minutes, all
three were trussed up like turkeys.

But of course,
when Jake reached the
Captain's cabin, there
was no Captain to
be seen.

"So," breathed Jake.
"Hidin' is 'ee, the
cowardly old blackguard! And it could be
dangerous trying to seek 'im out in the
dark. We'll lie up til mornin' . . . and
then, ah-harrrh . . . *we'll* sniff 'im out!"

So Jake and his men kept watch over
their captives and settled down to drink
rum and play cards, and sing very rude
sea-shanties until dawn. They had all
quite forgotten that the Captain had a
cabin boy called Tom.

On the island, Tom was
woken early by the singing.
"Not like our lot to sing
at this time o'day," he thought.
"I wonder what's up?"

He set out for a high rock on the point
to find out . . . and he saw quite a lot.

In the little bay on his left hand was Jake's
ship. "Help," thought Tom. "I'd know the
Flying Dustman anywhere."

Then, in the right-hand bay he saw Jake's
longboat tied up alongside the *Black Pig*.

"That's bad," he said to himself. "Jake
must have captured the ship! And *what* are
we going to do about *that*?"

So Tom thought and thought, and then
at last he had what seemed to be a good idea.

He went back to the dinghy . . . and unpacked a quantity of bacon and eggs from the stores.

Then he lit a fire back at the camp-site, and began to fry.

SIZZLE SIZZLE

Luckily, his plan worked. The breeze carried the delicious smell of cooking out towards the *Black Pig* . . .

. . . just as Jake and his men came out on deck to begin their search for the Captain.

"So *that's* where he's skulking!" roared Jake. "Man the longboat, me handsomes. Now we'll take that old booby, Pugwash . . . *and* his breakfast!"

And greedily he and his men tumbled
into their boat and set off for the island.

Meanwhile, Captain Pugwash was
awoken by the sound of sizzling and the
tempting smell . . .

but Tom said,
"This bacon's not for now. Quick!
Help me with the dinghy!"

And a moment later, he and the Captain were carrying the little boat to the other side of the point.

B-B-BUT... WH-WHAT...

SHH, CAP'N, KEEP YOUR HEAD DOWN!

Poor Captain Pugwash. It was bad enough to have lost his ship, but now, with his breakfast gone as well he began to feel quite sorry for himself. And of course he had no idea what was *really* happening.

For, just as Cut-throat Jake was beaching his longboat on one side of the point . . .

Tom, hidden from Jake on the other side, was setting out with the Captain in the dinghy . . .

and making (to Pugwash's surprise) *not* for the *Black Pig* . . .

but for *Jake*'s ship, the *Flying Dustman*!

"Now, Cap'n," said Tom, when they reached it. "Hold tight to the anchor chain . . . . I'm going to saw it through and cast the *Flying Dustman* adrift."

And very soon Tom had hacked through one of the rusty links. The chain fell away into the water, and if Tom hadn't grabbed him the Captain would have fallen in, too.

WHOOPS!

Then Tom started to row for all he was worth back towards the *Black Pig*.

In the meantime, on the island, Jake and his pirates had followed their noses to the camp-site, and were quarrelling greedily over the bacon and eggs.

In fact, they'd forgotten all about the man they were looking for . . .

until suddenly
Jake looked round
and saw . . .
to his amazement, horror and fury . . .

. . . Tom and the Captain climbing on board the *Black Pig* and his own *Flying Dustman* drifting away quite fast on the outgoing tide.

"AFTER THEM!" roared Jake, and he and his men rushed back to their longboat . . .

But by the time they were afloat
Tom had untied the Mate and Willy
and Barnabas and the *Black Pig* was
under way.

A fresh breeze sprang up, and although
Jake's pirates rowed like demons . . .

the *Black Pig* drew far
ahead of them as the
sails filled and she made
for the open sea.

In fact, the ship's wake caught Jake's
longboat, and pitched them all into the
water. They cursed and swore horribly,

but with their own ship drifting far
away on the horizon—there was nothing,

nothing at all that they could do about it
except swim miserably back to the island.

"And now," said Tom, when he felt it
was safe to hand over the steering wheel
to the Captain, "it really is breakfast time.
Bacon and eggs all round!"

"Hurrah!" cried the Mate.

"And no ship's biscuits,"
shouted Barnabas.

"Nor weevils, neither,"
added Willy.
"Poor little things!"

So, for the second time that morning
Tom cooked the breakfast . . .

. . . and very good it was too.

"Clever lad, our Tom!" said the Mate.

"Aye . . . worth 'is weight in gold,"
said Willy, munching happily.

"*Almost* worth having the Cap'n back,
to have Tom around!" remarked Barnabas.

But Pugwash didn't hear them.
"Fluttering flounders!" he cried, the
steering wheel in one hand and a forkful
of bacon in the other . . .

"You fellows didn't get very far without
your famous Captain—eh! Fussing about a
few mouldy biscuits indeed.

They soon needed me back when
there was *real* trouble afoot! . . .
eh, Tom lad? . . ."

But Tom was busy starting the
washing up . . . and he just smiled,
and said . . . nothing.

for Priscilla

PUGWASH
AND THE
FANCY-DRESS
PARTY

It was a pleasant sunny morning in
a busy English sea-port. On every
side was the hustle and bustle of the
harbour. There were ships of every
shape and size, but one in particular
attracted the attention of the crowd
for she had never been seen in that
town before.

It was Captain
Pugwash's ship, the
Black Pig.

She had sailed into the harbour
the night before . . .

and although she
looked well enough
outside . . .

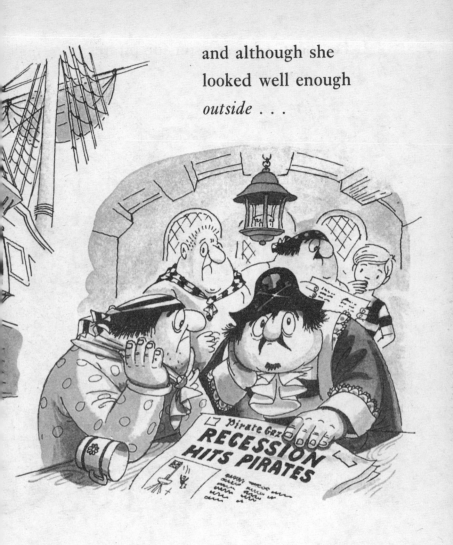

inside, the Captain and his crew
were in a state of deepest gloom.

It had been a bad season for pirates . . .

There was no treasure left in the
treasure-chest . . .

no food in the
ration-store . . .

no rum in the
rum–barrel.

"There isn't a smidge of gunpowder,"
said the Mate, "nor one single cannon ball!"

But at that, the Captain brightened.
"CANNON BALL!!" he cried.

"A *ball* . . . a party . . .
a Grand Ball . . .
a Fancy-dress Ball!
We'll have one on
board the ship—
with a trip round the
bay for good measure.

"We shall invite all the smartest and *richest* folk in town. They'll come in their finest clothes, gleaming with gold and silver . . .

dripping with diamonds and gems. And once they're on board – ho-ho! – we'll put a sleeping drug in their Rum Punch . . .

then . . . hee-hee . . . as we sail round the bay, they will all fall into a deep sleep! . . .

at which point, we strip them of
all their richest possessions . . . put
them ashore . . . and sail away as
wealthy as kings!"

The pirates all thought this was a
splendid plan. Only Tom the cabin boy
wasn't so sure. It seemed like daylight
robbery to him . . .

But Captain Pugwash was so pleased
with his plot that he actually took a

gold piece (which
he had pretended
he hadn't got)
out of his Black
Piggy-Bank . . .

and gave it to the pirates to buy food
and drink and bunting for the party.

Then he wrote
the invitations and
gave them to Tom
to deliver to all the
smartest addresses
in town.

And it was while he was doing this . . .

that Tom noticed *someone* on the way who
made him think of a quite different plan for
the Captain's Party . . .
so much so that
he dropped one
invitation accidentally
on purpose on
the pavement.

And . . . as Tom had hoped . . .

the *someone* picked
it up . . .

It was, of course, Cut-throat Jake, the Captain's worst enemy, who, with his band of wicked pirates just *happened* to be in the same town and had already observed that Pugwash was there too!

"Well, well, well," breathed Jake. "Now ain't that *real* generous of my old *friend* the Captain. A Ball on board ship . . .

The Captain and crew of the good ship BLACK PIG invite you to a GRAND BALL on SHIP this SATURDAY afternoon. A TRIP ROUND THE B... FANCY-DRE...

a trip round the Bay . . . and . . . Fancy-dress, eh?

We accept with pleasure! eh, my
beauties? . . . with *much* pleasure,
ho-ho-ho!"

When the morning of the Party came,
Tom got out the dressing-up box. The
Mate put on the uniform
of a footman.

Willy disguised himself
as a serving-maid.

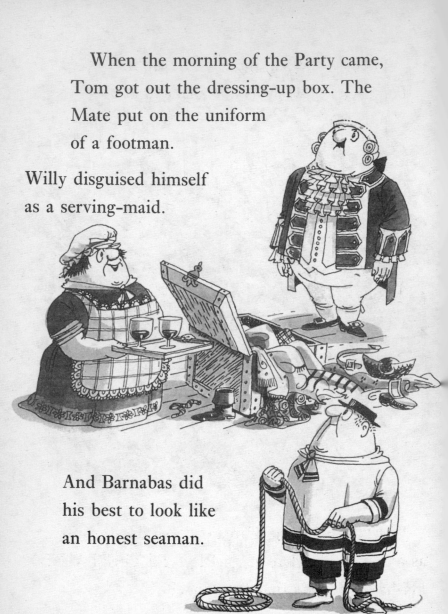

And Barnabas did
his best to look like
an honest seaman.

Then:— "What about you, Cap'n?" asked
Tom, for Pugwash hadn't changed at all.

"Ah!" replied the Captain, "*I'm* dressed up
as a . . . guess what . . . a PIRATE CAPTAIN.
Ha-ha . . . how's that for a joke?"

That afternoon, the guests began to arrive.

Everybody who was anybody was there . . .
masked, be-wigged and be-jewelled . . .

and all the people of the town
gathered to watch them go aboard.

As the Mate announced the titles,

the Captain could hardly believe his
good fortune!

Soon the deck was crowded with guests. Never had such a distinguished company gathered on board the *Black Pig*.

"Mix the Rum Punch, Tom!" cried the Captain. So Tom mixed it and Willy served it, and Captain Pugwash, careful to take none himself, rubbed his hands

with glee at the sight of all the riches
which would be his when the drink
began to take effect.

Then, just as the Captain was about
to give the order to sail, the Mate cried,
"Wait! There's one more party to
come aboard!"

And sure enough, the strangest group, wearing tall black hats and masks and cloaks held high to conceal their faces, came striding up the gang-plank.

SO FAR SO GOOD!

"Maybe they'll prove the richest of the lot beneath all that disguise," thought the Captain to himself.

Then:— "Anchors aweigh!" he shouted.
"Forward Miss Willy! Extra-special drinks
for our mystery guests."

So Tom mixed up some more of the
Rum Punch, and indeed it was extra-special.
Then, as the newcomers thirstily swallowed
it all up . . .

the ship sailed
out of the
harbour . . .

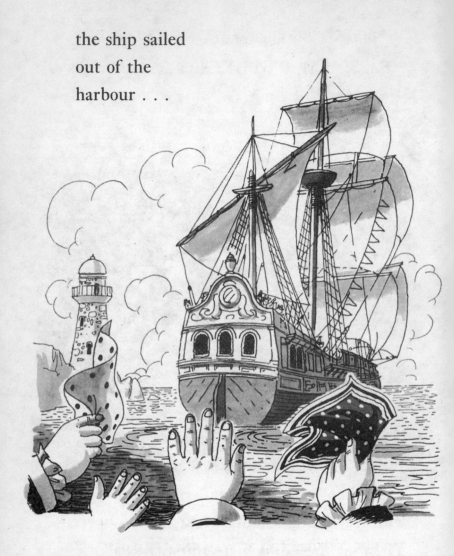

the crowds waved them good-bye . . .

and the guests settled down to enjoy
the Ball.

Tom played merrily on his
concertina, and it was not until the
ship rounded the lighthouse . . .

that a terrible
voice shouted,
"UNMASK, ME
HANDSOMES!"
Then off came
the black hats
and masks, and
in a moment . . .

Pugwash and his crew and his guests
found themselves confronted and surrounded . . .

by Cut-throat Jake and his bloodthirsty band!

"Right! Grab
the loot!!" roared
Cut-throat Jake.
His wicked eye
glinted and his
great black beard bristled with greed
as he watched his villainous blackguards

snatching the Duchess's diamonds, the
Mayor's chain of office . . .

rings, necklaces and bracelets,

silver watches and purses of gold galore!

Soon a great heap of booty lay in the middle of the deck. Jake chuckled with glee and addressed the guests.

"Much obliged, I'm sure," he growled.

"And now, in return for your – er – *generosity* – I'm goin' to set 'ee all adrift in the longboat, while *we* make our get-away in this 'ere 'andsome vessel!

"But as for *you*, you scurvy lot," he snarled, turning on Pugwash and his crew. "You what 'as contributed *nothing* to the Cut-throat Jake Benefit Fund . . .

I'll waste no longboat on *your* worthless skins! You'll walk the plank every one of you!" And then, suddenly, even as he spoke . . .

Jake blinked, swayed and staggered . . .

BONK·K·K!

and fell flat on his back in a
dead faint on the deck—

and all his crew did the same!

Captain Pugwash was astonished. Why had only Jake and his men suffered from the drugged drinks?

But then he realised that all the guests were cheering, and they were cheering HIM! They didn't know, of course, that Pugwash had intended to rob *them*. They thought he'd arranged to drug Jake's drinks to save them! Least of all did they know that it was all Tom's doing!

"Bravo, Captain!" cried the Mayor.
"Very quick thinking on your part!"

"Dashed fine show," said Sir Splycemeigh-Maynebrace. "The skill and speed with which you dealt with those dreadful desperadoes has saved us all!"

Then the guests recovered their stolen
possessions, and the *Black Pig* sailed back
into the harbour again.
And Jake and
his crew, awake
now, but in
irons . . .

were marched away to the deepest
dungeons of the town gaol.

"And now, Captain," said the Mayor when the guests had dispersed to their homes. "What can we do to reward you for all *you* have done for us?"

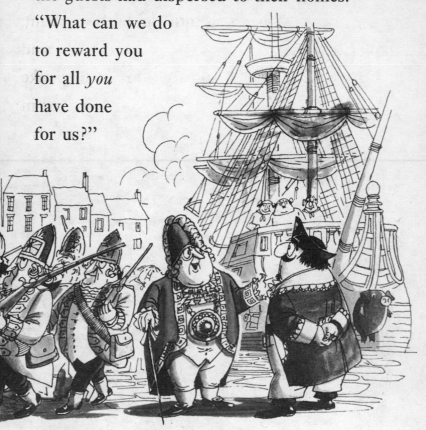

"Well, since you mention it, there *are* one or two little things we could do with," replied the Captain.

"A few ships' stores, perhaps. Provisions—
rum, cannon balls and gunpowder so that
we may set sail again and go about our
honest trade!"

"It shall be done," said the Mayor.

And the next day, the Mayor himself
came to supervise the delivery of all the
supplies the Captain had asked for.

There was even a handsome cash present
for Pugwash himself to mark the skill and
presence of mind with which he had
disposed of Cut-throat Jake and his band.

"Why fancy that, Captain," said the
Mayor, as he shook him warmly by the
hand. "You're *still* wearing your fancy-dress!"

"Suffering sea-snakes! So I am!"
cried the Captain. "Young Tom ought to
have reminded me! Not very bright, that
cabin boy of mine!"

And Tom smiled as he listened to the
Captain's remarks,

but he said nothing.

PUGWASH
AND THE MIDNIGHT FEAST

PUGWASH
AND THE WRECKERS

John Ryan

"Havin' a midnight feast, eh?" roared Jake, "and never thought of askin' *us* to join you?"

Captain Pugwash and his crew are interrupted eating their midnight feast by some very unwelcome visitors – Cut-throat Jake and his bloodthirsty buccaneers! The greedy villains take over, but not for long...And there's more crafty plotting from the evil Jake when he sets out to wreck the *Black Pig*, full of the biggest load of bullion ever!

Also in Young Puffin

ADVENTURE ON

SKULL

ISLAND

Tony Bradman

Life for a pirate family is one long adventure!

When Jim finds a treasure map of Skull Island on board the *Saucy Sally*, he knows he and his sister Molly are in for an exciting time. But little do they know that their great enemy, Captain Swagg, is after the same treasure – and is determined to get there first!

MYSTERY AT MUSKET BAY

Tony Bradman

"Ghosts and graveyards! Ghosts and graveyards!"

Trelawney the parrot is certain Dead Man's Island is haunted. He won't stop squawking about it! But the rest of the Bluebeard family think there might be more to the mystery of Musket Bay when they find strange footprints in the sand. Would a real ghost leave footprints?

Also in Young Puffin

Peril at the Pirate School

Tony Bradman

Miss Prudence Proper was tall and bony, and she had a big hooked nose. There were a couple of hairy warts right on the end of it. Some of her teeth were missing, some were green, and the rest were black.

Molly and Jim have been sent to Miss Prudence Proper's Academy for Pirate Pupils. But even for a pirate school, the teachers are very strange. Soon Jim is in deadly danger. Can Molly save him? What is *really* happening at the school?